The Knight, the Princess & the Magic Rock

A Classic Persian Tale

Retold by

Sara Azizi

Illustrated by

Alireza Sadeghian

✦Wisdom Tales✦

Wisdom Tales is an imprint of World Wisdom, Inc. Book Design by Stephen Williams.
Library of Congress Cataloging-in-Publication Data
Azizi, Sara, 1977- The knight, the princess & the magic rock : a classic Persian tale / retold by Sara Azizi ; illustrated by Alireza Sadeghian.   p. cm. Summary: While on a mission for his king, a brave young Persian knight falls in love with a beautiful princess, daughter of the neighboring king, who is an enemy of Persia. ISBN 978-1-937786-01-4 (hardcover : alk. paper) [1. Folklore--Iran.] I. Sadeghian, Alireza, 1980- ill. II. Title. III. Title: Knight, the princess, and the magic rock.   PZ8.1.A95Kni 2012   398.20955--dc23   [E] 2012002046
Printed in China on acid-free paper
Production Date: 2/14/2012; Plant & Location: Printed by Everbest Printing Co., Ltd., Nansha, China; Job/Batch #: 103810
For information address Wisdom Tales. P.O. Box 2682, Bloomington, Indiana 47402-2682
www.wisdomtalespress.com

Background

The Knight, the Princess & the Magic Rock is a love story featured in the *Shāhnāmeh,* or "Book of Kings," written in around 1000 A.D. by the Persian poet Ferdowsī. This famous work, comprised of 60,000 verses, is the national epic of Greater Persia and tells the story of the mythical past of Iran from the creation of the world until the Islamic conquest of Persia in the 7th century.

In the *Shāhnāmeh*, Bijan (pronounced bee-jan) was a young warrior during the reign of Kai Khosrow. During a mission to help the people on the northern frontiers of Persia rid their farms of the invading wild boars, he fell in love with Manijeh (pronounced ma-nee-jeh), the daughter of Afrāsiāb, king of Tūrān, and the greatest enemy of Persia. Bijan was imprisoned by Afrāsiāb, forcing Kai Khosrow to send the legendary hero Rostam, disguised as a merchant, to save Bijan.

This adapted version of the story of Bijan and Manijeh is based on the commentary of Adham Khalkhālī, a Sufi or Islamic mystic who died in 1642 A.D.

The Knight, the Princess & the Magic Rock

A Classic Persian Tale

Gather about, my grandchildren, and listen closely,

while I tell you the wondrous story of

Bijan and Manijeh.

Once upon a time

in the ancient land of Persia. . .

2

a great king ruled with kindness and justice. One day, some farmers came to the king and told him about wild boars that were destroying their farms. The king listened to their pleas and promised to help them.

4

The king called for Bijan, a brave young knight, and told him to help the farmers. Bijan mounted his horse and left without delay. He rode day and night until he reached the place.

There he found the boars, and he drove them off to a faraway land so that they would not return to harm the farms. Confident that he had finished his mission for the king, *Bijan* set off for home.

On his way back home, Bijan passed by a beautiful garden and there he caught sight of the most beautiful maiden he had ever seen. She, too, saw him and they fell in love. Who was she? She was Manijeh, princess of the kingdom that was an enemy to Persia! But this did not matter to Bijan, who was in love. They enjoyed their time together in the beautiful garden, but when Manijeh had to return to her father, the king of Turan, she could not bear parting with Bijan…

She came up with a plan. She gave Bijan a magic potion which caused him to sleep, and then she had him secretly carried away to her father's palace on a covered palanquin. When Bijan awoke, he found himself in his enemy's fortress, though he did not care so long as he and Manijeh were together.

But secrets are hard to keep, and soon Bijan was discovered. The king of Turan was furious. He ordered his guards to imprison Bijan in a distant pit that was dug deep into the ground. They closed the opening of the pit with a magic rock that no one could lift.

Manijeh, too, suffered for having hidden Bijan. As her punishment, she was banished from the palace. She had lost both her home and her beloved Bijan.

She knew she could not live without Bijan. She searched and searched until finally she found the pit. But no matter how hard she tried, she could not move the rock. Eventually she found a small opening near the base of the boulder. Through this hole she lowered food down to Bijan. "Help will come," thought Manijeh hopefully, "Bijan must survive."

Back in Persia, the king wondered why his knight had not returned. Now, the king had a golden cup in which he could see all the corners

of the world. He prayed all night long and then looked into his cup and saw all that had happened to Bijan.

17

It would be hard to rescue Bijan. Someone must go to the land of the enemy and bring him back. "Only one man," thought the king, "is able to do this: Rostam, the bravest of all knights." So the king immediately sent his messenger to summon him.

Rostam was the king's most trusted knight. He was strong and wise and, for as long as anyone could remember, it had been his power that had protected the king.

19

Rostam was sad to hear the news, but he soon thought of a plan.

20

He left for the land of the enemy with his men, all wearing merchants' robes, and he took with him a hundred camels carrying goods and treasures.

When they came to the enemy's country, Rostam searched for Bijan in secret but could not find him. When Manijeh heard that merchants from Persia had arrived in the city, she went to see them. She learned why they had come and told them where Bijan could be found.

22

Rostam listened to Manijeh's story. He felt sorry for her and comforted her. As Manijeh was leaving, he gave her some food for Bijan, but in the food he hid his ring.

When Bijan found the ring and saw the name of Rostam on the ring, his heart was filled with hope and joy. He told Manijeh who Rostam really was. Then, when night fell, Manijeh built a big fire by the pit so that Rostam and his men could find it.

When Rostam and his men reached the pit, they discovered that not one of them could move the rock, no matter how hard they tried. Rostam then realized that only the power of prayer would be able to overcome the magic of the rock. He put all of his heart and mind into his prayer and then . . . he was able to move the rock aside. Bijan was saved!

Rostam and his men returned triumphantly to Persia with Bijan and Manijeh. They all went to the king and told him everything. They told him how Bijan, who had been thrown into prison because of Manijeh, had also been saved by her. "You must love and treasure Manijeh with all your heart, for she has suffered for you and has saved you," the king said to Bijan.

Soon, Bijan and Manijeh were married, and they lived happily ever after, and their love for each other grew and grew. . .

29

And that is the story of *Bijan* and his *Manijeh*.

"How wonderful!" said the children. "Grandfather, do you know any other stories?"

"I do indeed, but they will have to wait for another day."

Interpreting the Story

Because the story of Bijan and Manijeh is so rich in symbolism, it can be understood on many levels, which is one reason why it has been so treasured in Persia for centuries. Young children will certainly enjoy the simple adventure story, but as they grow older, they may appreciate its deeper meanings, too. It has long been interpreted as an extended parable by generations of spiritual teachers and students in Persia.

One possible spiritual interpretation is as follows: the earthly king and his kingdom represent the Lord and His heavenly realm. The king sends Bijan, who represents humankind, to resist and overcome evil in the world. By successfully ridding the land of the boars, Bijan conquers outward evil and thinks himself victorious; however, since he has not vanquished all evil within himself, he falls prey to the temptation of the world. At first, Manijeh represents the world in its seductive aspect: her beauty hypnotizes Bijan and makes him forget his mission; thus he becomes a prisoner of a lower world that is ignorant of the Lord. The rock cutting him off from the heavenly light above represents the obstruction of the self-centered ego. However, the world that tempts souls away from God can also bring them back to Him. Therefore through Manijeh, who now embodies creation in its *positive* aspect, Bijan not only survives but also meets his savior, Rostam. The great knight Rostam represents the divine emissary, who by God's will has descended to the world to aid humankind. The beauty which was the original cause of Bijan's downfall thus becomes an occasion for his rising up to God. Rostam disguises himself as a merchant, meaning that the divine representative "clothes" himself as a human being when descending into the world. The name of Rostam brings hope to the imprisoned Bijan and is like a promise of salvation. The fact that only Rostam is able to lift the rock signifies that humankind can be saved only with the assistance of God's chosen representative. Bijan's return to the kingdom and his marriage to Manijeh represent the self-purification and spiritual rebirth that restore us to our original nature that is "made in God's image."

Other Children's Books from Wisdom Tales

All Our Relatives: Traditional Native American Thoughts about Nature
by Paul Goble, 2005

The Boy and His Mud Horses: & Other Stories from the Tipi
by Paul Goble, 2010

*A Christmas Reader: Biblical Selections with Illustrations
from Around the World*
edited by Catherine Schuon and Michael Oren Fitzgerald, 2012

The Conference of the Birds
as told by Alexis York Lumbard, illustrated by Demi, 2012

The Earth Made New: Plains Indian Stories of Creation
by Paul Goble, 2009

Everyone Prays
by Alexis York Lumbard, illustrated by Demi, 2013

The Fantastic Adventures of Krishna
by Demi, 2013

Living in Two Worlds: The American Indian Experience
by Charles Eastman, edited by Michael Oren Fitzgerald, 2010

The Man Who Dreamed of Elk-Dogs: & Other Stories from the Tipi
by Paul Goble, 2012

Saint Francis of Assisi
by Demi, 2012

Tipi: Home of the Nomadic Buffalo Hunters
by Paul Goble, 2007

The Women Who Lived with Wolves: & Other Stories from the Tipi
by Paul Goble, 2011

www.wisdomtalespress.com